Hide-and-seek

Jaap Tuinman

CONSULTANTS

Sharon Anderson
Elaine Crocker
Maxine Bone
Jill Hamilton
Diana Hill
Orysia Hull
Sandy Johnstone
Moira Juliebö
Helen Langford
Mary Neeley
Carol Pfaff
Sharon Rich

PROGRAM EDITOR

Kathleen Doyle

GINN

Ginn Publishing Canada Inc.

JOURNEYS

Hide-and-seek
Emergent Level Two

C99122
0-7702-1667-6

Printed and bound in Canada.

CDEFGH 97654321

EDITORS
Sharon Stewart
Anne MacInnes

EDITORIAL CONSULTANT
Nicki Scrimger

ART/DESIGN
Sandi Meland Cherun/
Word & Image Design Studio

Contents

Are You There?

by Susan Green
Illustrated by Maryann Kovalski

Rosie, Rosie,
Are you there?
I can't find you
Anywhere.

Are you hiding under the porch?

Are you hiding in the barn?

Rosie, Rosie,
Are you there?
I can't find you
Anywhere.

Are you hiding behind the tractor?

Are you hiding up in the tree?

Rosie, Rosie,
Are you there?
I can't find you
Anywhere.

There you are.
I found you!

I Like to Play

by Sharon Stewart
Illustrated by Olena Kassian

I like to play leapfrog—
springing, bounding,
vaulting, landing.

I like to play hide-and-seek—
creeping, sneaking,
crouching, peeking.

I like to play hockey—
dashing, passing,
shooting, scoring.

I like to play baseball—
swinging, hitting,
running, sliding.

I like to play tricks—
teasing, fooling,
giggling, joking!